The Glassmaker's Daughter

Written by Dianne Hofmeyr

Illustrated by Jane Ray

Frances Lincoln
Children's Books

For Niki and Jude Daly – D.H.

For my dear friend Sita Brahmachari, with love – J.R.

First published in the Great Britain and the USA in 2017 by Frances Lincoln Children's Books,
an imprint of The Quarto Group, 142 W 36th Street, 4th Floor, New York, NY 10018, USA
QuartoKnows.com
Visit our blogs at QuartoKids.com

Important: there are age restrictions for most blogging and social media sites and in many countries parental consent is also required. Always ask permission from your parents. Website information is correct at time of going to press. However, the publishers cannot accept liability for any information or links found on any Internet sites, including third-party websites.

Text copyright © Dianne Hofmeyr 2017
Illustrations copyright © Jane Ray 2017

The right of Dianne Hofmeyr and Jane Ray to be identified as the author
and illustrator respectively of this work has been asserted by them in accordance
with the Copyright, Designs and Patents Act, 1988 (United Kingdom).

A catalogue record for this book is available from the British Library. LOC number pending

ISBN 978-1-84780-676-5

Illustrated with watercolour, gouache and ink
Designed by Andrew Watson and Karissa Santos
Edited by Katie Cotton and Kate Davies

Printed in China
1 3 5 7 9 8 6 4 2

The Glassmaker's Daughter

Written by Dianne Hofmeyr

Illustrated by Jane Ray

In Venice, recipes for making glass were kept closely guarded. A guild for glassmakers, the 'Ars Fiolaria', was started in 1224. Glassmakers became so important, they were allowed to carry swords and their daughters married into Venice's wealthiest families. But there was a catch – glassmakers were not allowed to leave the city in case their secret recipes were passed on to other cities and countries.

'Looking' glass was made by covering a flat sheet of glass with a thin layer of silver, mercury and tin – sometimes even with gold, which made the reflection more beautiful. There was a separate guild for looking-glass makers that made sure the recipe for making mirror remained secret.

There was once a beautiful city built on water.
Its palaces floated like birds in nests on the sea and
its lamplight danced like fireflies across the ripples.

Daniela, the glassmaker's daughter, lived in this shimmering city surrounded by delicate glass made in her father's furnace. Yet despite all this beauty, Daniela was a melancholy girl. She lay next to the canal all day long, scowling into the water – gloomy, glum and bored.

In despair her father
announced, 'I'll give a glass
palace to the person who can
make my daughter smile.'

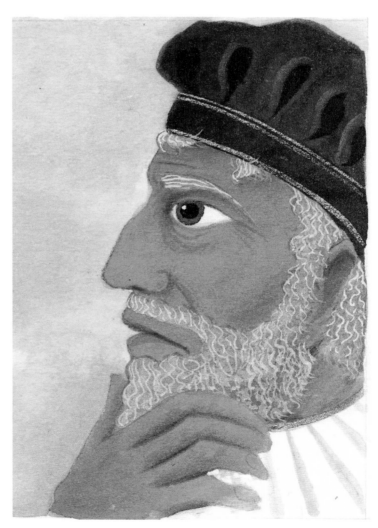

So his glass-blowers set to work. They blew
and pulled and pinched the molten glass into
silver-spun walls with pineapple-topped
turrets and winged-dragon doors.

News soon spread of the silver-spun
palace and people came from
far and wide to compete for
Daniela's smile.

First to arrive was
Maestro Barbagelata.
'Regard this!' he said as he blew
fiery rings of flame into the air.

He swallowed swords and even
snakes and almost turned himself
inside out with his tricks on a
tightrope. But instead of exciting
Daniela, she was gloomier than ever.

Then the most
famous of mask makers,
Donna Violetta Rufina Zangara,
arrived with a cabinet of masks – moons and stars and
suns, one a nest of twigs with tiny jewel-encrusted birds'
eggs, another a mermaid's lair lined with shells and pearls.

'Try these! They'll bring a smile to your face,' said Donna Violetta Rufina Zangara, holding up the smiliest of all her masks. But instead of delighting Daniela, she was glummer than ever.

Then Leonardo Leonino Grandi arrived. 'Behold this!' he cried.

He swept aside the curtain of his gondola. A HUGE lion jumped up with such a roar that the gondola rocked. Leonardi Leonini Grandi swayed… then fell backwards into the canal with an almighty splash, the lion on top of him.

But even this didn't bring a smile to Daniela's lips.

Glove makers, tart bakers, trumpet players, dragon slayers, monkey trickers, pocket pickers, bell ringers, opera singers – even sausage stringers – all failed to make Daniela smile.

'What's to be done?' her father groaned.
'How will such a miserable girl *ever* find happiness?'

But one young glassmaker
longed more than anyone to make Daniela
smile. In a corner of the workshop, Angelo
drew a molten globe from the furnace and
blew a bubble of glass.
'Flux and fire,' he whispered.
Then he snipped the bubble and laid it flat
and smoothed on slivers of silver mercury.
'Mercury and tin,' he chanted.
Then he rubbed the slivers down
with a hare's paw.
'Foiled and finished. And polished thin.'
Then he sang his secret song again.

*'Flux and fire. Mercury and tin.
Foiled and finished. And polished thin.'*

The other glassmakers peered across at him.

'What are you making, Angelo?'

'A gift that will make Daniela smile.'

'She hasn't smiled for an alchemist, an acrobat, an opera singer or a sausage stringer – why should she smile for you?'

Angelo ignored them all and went looking for Daniela.
He held out his gift.

'Glass? I don't need glass!' She pushed it aside.

'Look again, Principessa. This is no ordinary piece of
glass. It's different. Look *into* it.'

Daniela scowled as she held it up to her face.

'What do you see?' Angelo asked.

'I see a creature with a mouth like an upside-down slice of lemon and the eyes of a cross dragon.'

'Look again.'

She peered back at the glass. 'It's the funniest face in the world.'

Then the face started to change.

The frown lines disappeared.

The eyes sparkled.

The mouth turned up.

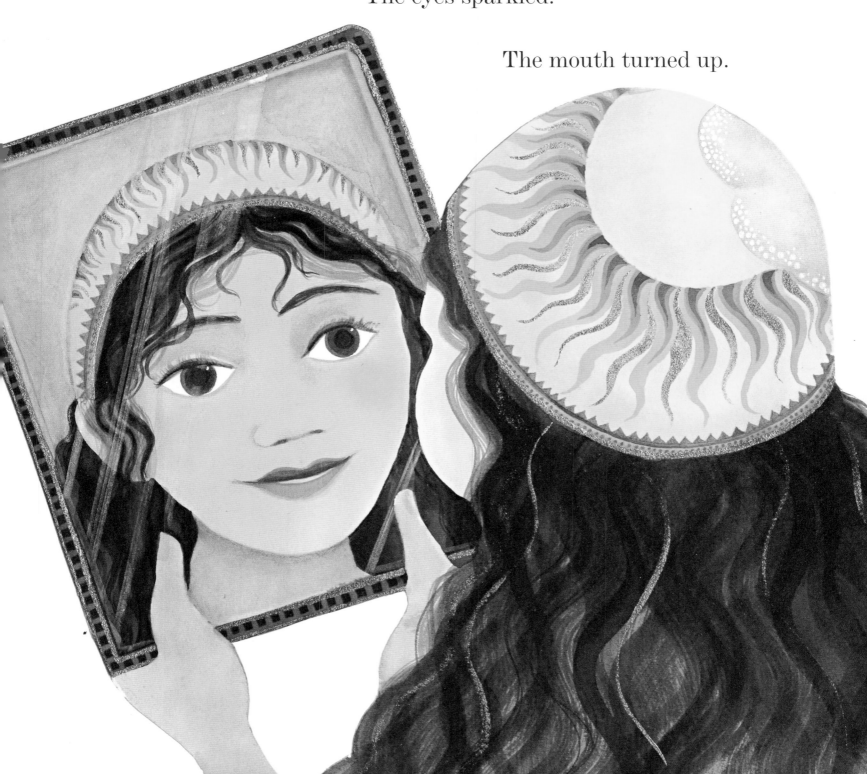

Daniela burst out laughing.
And the more she looked at the person
in the glass, the more she laughed.
At each fresh peal of laughter, glass began to shiver
and tinkle around her.

The palace quivered.

A pineapple snapped off a turret and came tumbling down.

The silver-spun walls splintered.

There was a sound of CRACKING...

SHATTERING...

SPLINTERING...

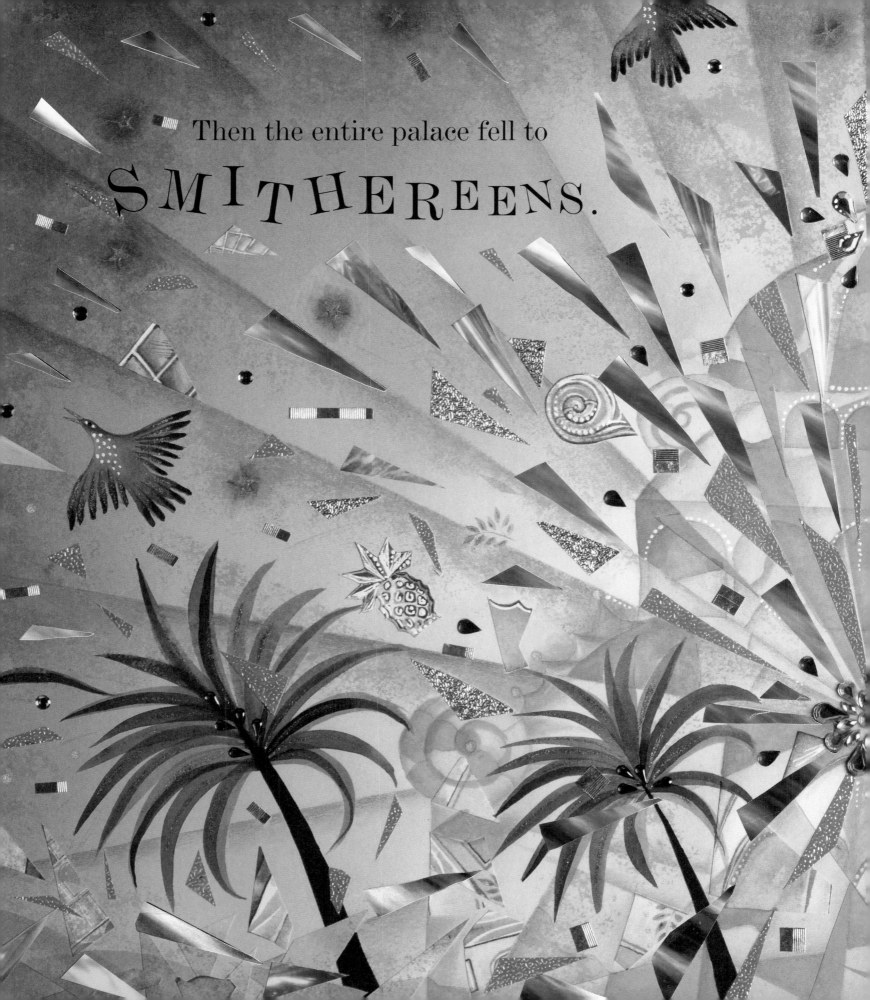

Then the entire palace fell to
SMITHEREENS.

Daniela's father rushed forward. 'Angelo, I'll build you another palace, but tell me your secret. How did your magic glass change my daughter?'
Angelo shook his head. 'She changed herself. My glass only reflects what's already there. Happiness is inside all of us. You only have to discover it.'

Daniela couldn't stop herself from peeping into the glass and laughing again. 'You're right. I found it by looking at my gloomy, grumpy face. I don't need mask makers, tart bakers, trumpet players, dragon slayers, bell ringers, or even sausage stringers to make me happy.'

And she laughed with such delight that the glass pieces at her feet started tinkling.

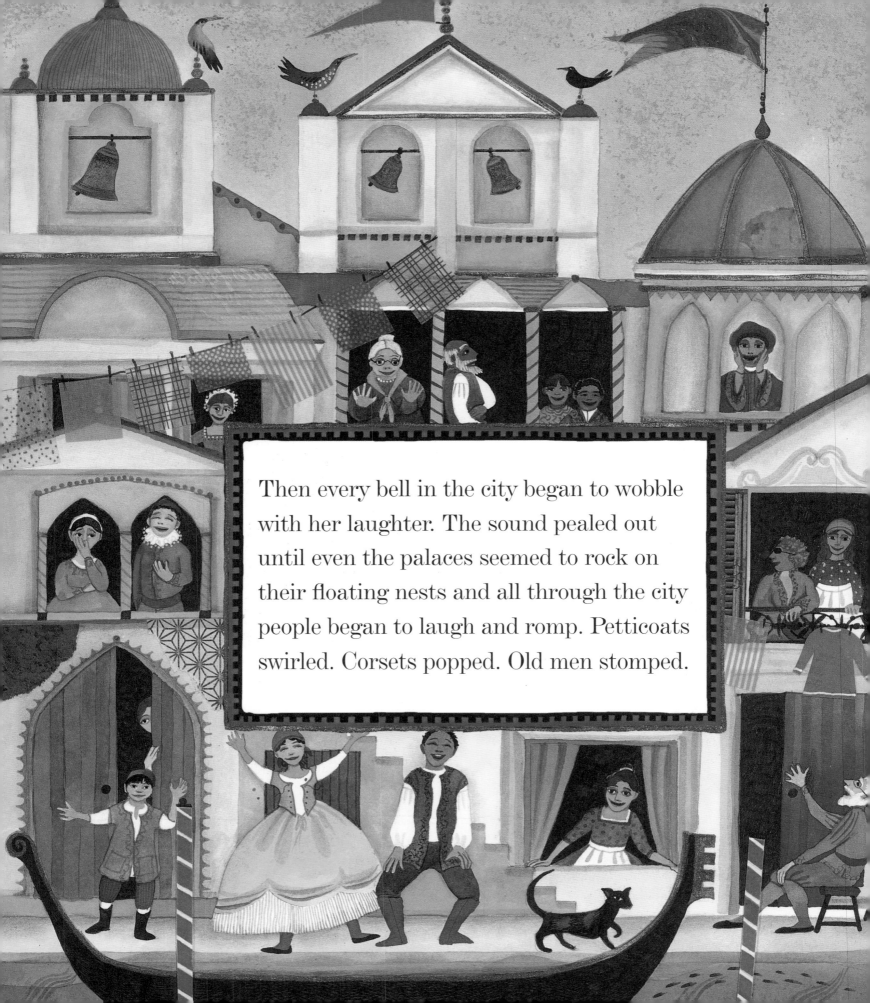

Then every bell in the city began to wobble with her laughter. The sound pealed out until even the palaces seemed to rock on their floating nests and all through the city people began to laugh and romp. Petticoats swirled. Corsets popped. Old men stomped.

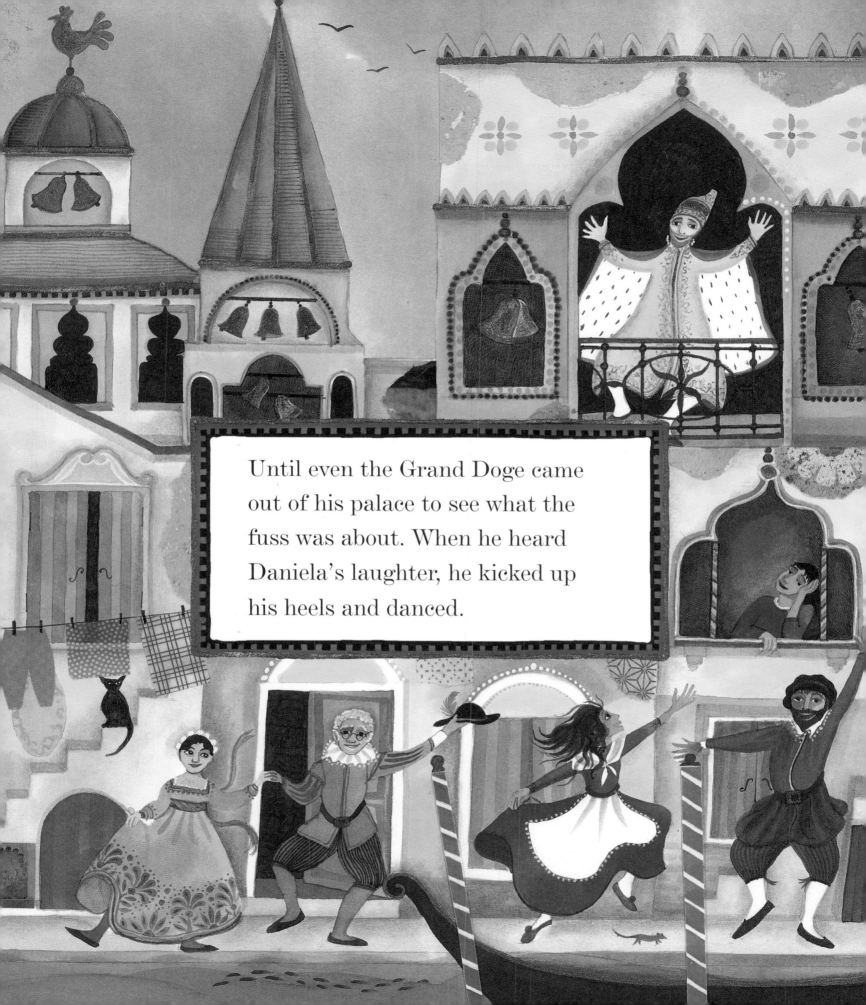

Until even the Grand Doge came out of his palace to see what the fuss was about. When he heard Daniela's laughter, he kicked up his heels and danced.

So now when you hear the bells of Venice ringing out
over the water, you can be sure Daniela is laughing.
And don't be surprised if you peep into a looking glass
to find a small smile creeping across your face.